For Jess xxx —C. H.

For Les —E. U.

BLOOMSBURY CHILDREN'S BOOKS
Bloomsbury Publishing Inc., part of Bloomsbury Publishing Plc
1385 Broadway, New York, NY 10018

BLOOMSBURY, BLOOMSBURY CHILDREN'S BOOKS, and the Diana logo
are trademarks of Bloomsbury Publishing Plc

First published in Great Britain in August 2018 by Bloomsbury Publishing Plc
Published in the United States of America in July 2019
by Bloomsbury Children's Books

Text copyright © 2018 by Caryl Hart
Illustrations copyright © 2018 by Edward Underwood

Bloomsbury books may be purchased for business or promotional use. For information on bulk purchases please contact
Macmillan Corporate and Premium Sales Department at specialmarkets@macmillan.com

Library of Congress Cataloging-in-Publication Data
Names: Hart, Caryl, author. | Underwood, Edward (Illustrator), illustrator.
Title: One shoe two shoes / by Caryl Hart ; illustrated by Edward Underwood.
Description: New York : Bloomsbury, 2019.
Summary: Introduces colors and the numbers one to ten as increasing
numbers of mice explore a wide variety of shoes.
Identifiers: LCCN 2018045842 (print) • LCCN 2018051389 (e-book)
ISBN 978-1-5476-0094-6 (hardcover) • ISBN 978-1-5476-0095-3 (e-book) • ISBN 978-1-5476-0096-0 (e-PDF)
Subjects: | CYAC: Shoes—Fiction. | Mice—Fiction. | Color—Fiction. | Counting—Fiction.
Classification: LCC PZ7.H25633 One 2019 (print) | LCC PZ7.H25633 (e-book) | DDC [E]—dc23
LC record available at https://lccn.loc.gov/2018045842

Art created with pencil, ink, and computer-assisted collage
Typeset in Filosofia
Book design by Goldy Broad
Printed in China by Leo Paper Products, Heshan, Guangdong
2 4 6 8 10 9 7 5 3 1

All papers used by Bloomsbury Publishing Plc are natural, recyclable products
made from wood grown in well-managed forests. The manufacturing processes
conform to the environmental regulations of the country of origin.

To find out more about our authors and books visit www.bloomsbury.com and sign up for our newsletters.

One Shoe
Two Shoes

illustrated by

Caryl Hart

Edward Underwood

BLOOMSBURY
CHILDREN'S BOOKS
NEW YORK LONDON OXFORD NEW DELHI SYDNEY

One shoe

Two shoes

Red shoes

Blue shoes

Old shoes

New shoes

On their way to school shoes

Long laces tied in knots

Green pumps
with yellow spots

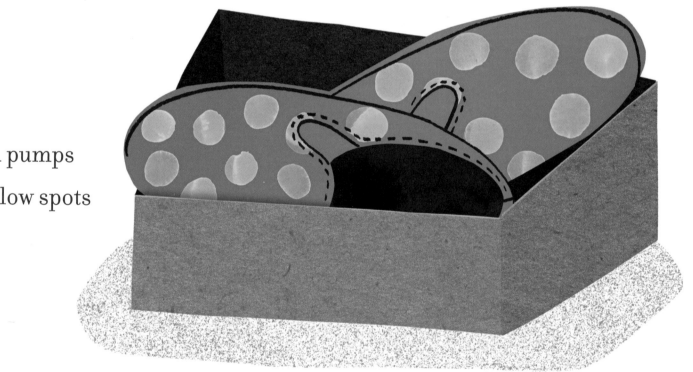

Party shoes

Artsy shoes

Cowboy boots

Flip-flops!

Two shoes make a pair.

Who's that hiding there?

Little mouse one
and little mouse two!

They've made a house
in someone's shoe!

A shoe

for a *house*?

A house

for a *mouse*?

Mouse's houses,

red and blue.

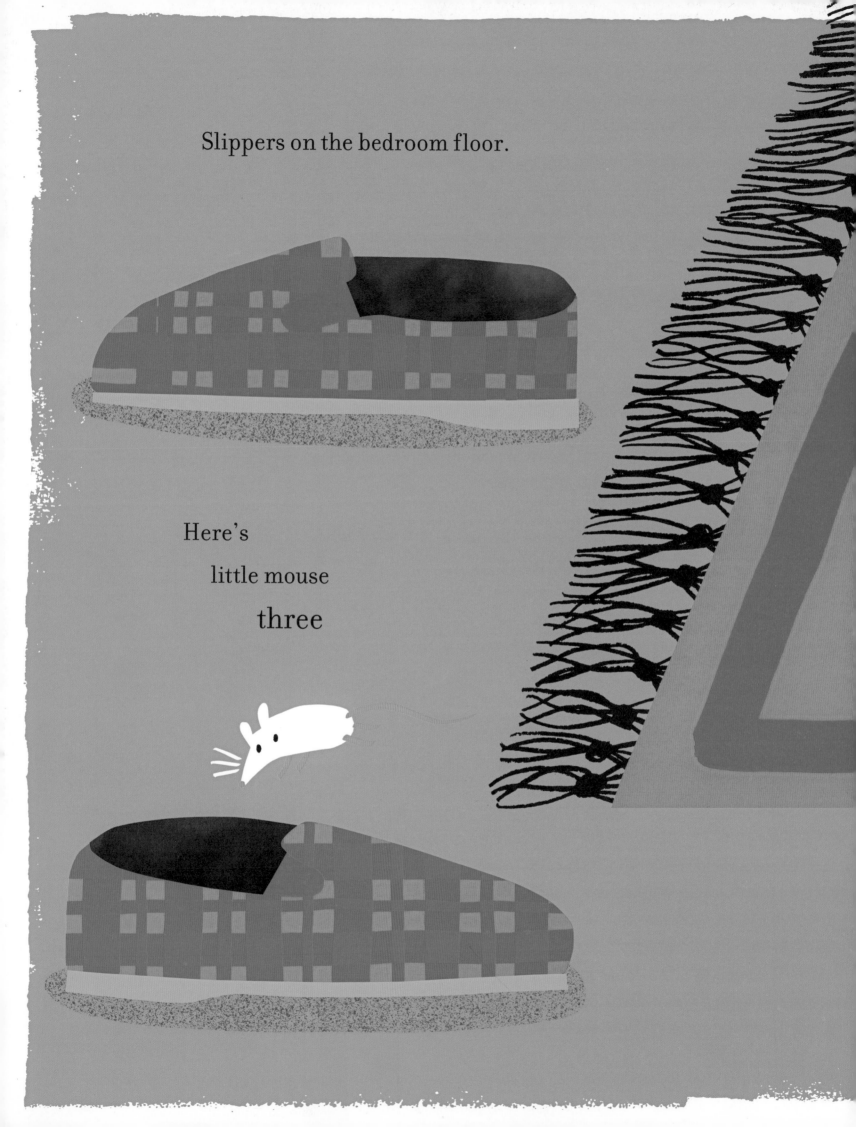

Slippers on the bedroom floor.

Here's
little mouse
three

and little mouse four!

Five

six

seven

eight and nine

ten little white mice

all in line!

Scritchy scratchy

Who goes there?

Pitter

Patter

Sniff

Lick

SCATTER!

Doggy s t r e t c h

Good boy—
fetch!

Bounce away

Time to play

Hooray!